JACK'S MEGA MACHINES
THE ROCKET RACING CAR

Alison Ritchie and Mike Byrne

SIMON AND SCHUSTER

London   New York   Sydney   Toronto   New Delhi

Mechanic Jack was up early at Rally Road workshop. He had a very special car to mend – a TURBOCHARGED racing car! Jack was the best mechanic for miles around. He could fix anything.

THE ROCKET RACING CAR

In no time he had mended a dent in the wing, fixed the steering and polished the bodywork. The car was ready for a test drive!

Rally Road workshop was magic. Every time Jack drove out through the doors, he had a thrilling adventure! "OK, Riley, hop in," he told his dog. Riley barked and wagged his tail.

Jack started the engine—

With a loud CLUNK the workshop doors flew open

and the shiny red car zoomed off into . . .

"Wow! Just look at this!" Jack chuckled.

The racing car whizzed higher and higher, zig-zagging

between planets, until Jack spotted a flashing sign . . .

WELCOME TO
THE INTERGALACTIC
SPACE RACE!

"A proper space race!" gasped Jack. "Let's go!"
With a screech of brakes, he landed the car inside a stadium.

It was packed with space vehicles and swarming with aliens
of every shape and size – spiky, slimy and spotty ones, long
pointy ones and small, round wobbly ones.

Jack couldn't believe his eyes.

Just then, a two-headed creature charged over.
"You're just in time!" he said. "The race is about to begin,
and we are one car short! Quick – follow me!"

Before Jack had time to catch his breath, he found himself at the start line between a spotty spacecab and an ENORMOUS milky way monster truck.

Jack gulped nervously as five sets of red lights went on one by one
to signal the start of the race . . .

KERPOW!

He pressed down hard on the accelerator pedal and
the rocket racing car blasted off like a torpedo.

Jack and Riley whizzed past moon buggies, hovercarts and comet-crawlers.
Riley barked in excitement. They were in second place!

But just as they were about to
overtake the monster truck . . .

it skidded straight off the track!

Jack pulled over. The sad-looking alien cried, "My tyres have burst!"
"Don't worry, I'll help you," said Jack.

Once they'd fixed all ten tyres,
Jack jumped into the rocket racing car
and tore off back into the race.

There was a lot of ground to make up
but if any car could catch up, this car could!

Jack was right behind the spotty spacecab when it started to spin around.

"You've got a problem with your steering!" he shouted. "I'll help!"

He screeched to a stop and
grabbed a spanner from his toolbox.

He mended the spacecab in a jiffy.
Soon they were both hurtling along the track again!

Jack zoomed up alongside a galactic go-kart.

He was about to overtake when suddenly a cloud of smoke filled the air. Jack flashed his warning lights, then leaped out of his car and ran over.

"The engine is overheating. You'll have to let it cool down," he told the little Martian. "Why don't you finish the race in the red racing car with us?"

Back on the circuit, the rocket car was so far behind, Jack could hardly see the other racers. "We'll never catch up!" moaned the Martian. Riley wagged his tail to cheer him up, and knocked a big red button on the dashboard.

WOOOOOSH

The rocket racing car took off at supersonic speed and began to streak past all the other racers!

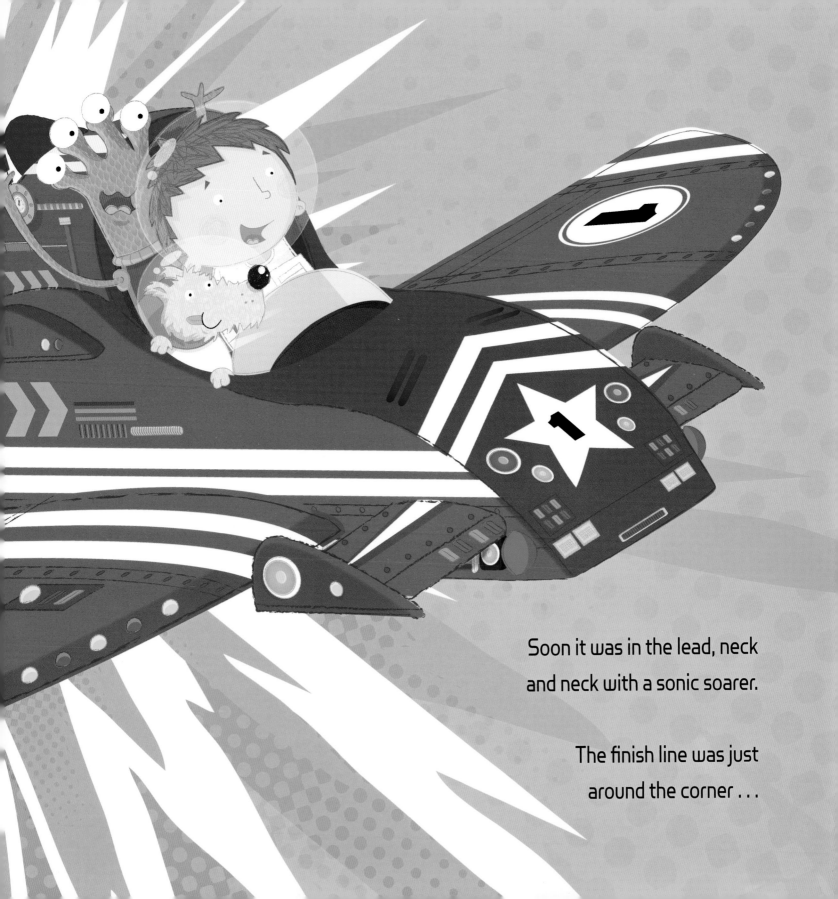

Soon it was in the lead, neck and neck with a sonic soarer.

The finish line was just around the corner . . .

The black and white flag came down. The rocket racing
car and the sonic soarer flew over the line together.
But who was the winner? It was a photo finish!

Jack waited anxiously for the green alien to announce the result.
At last, he picked up his megaphone. "This was the closest race ever!"
he said. "But the photo finish confirms that by a nanosecond,
the winner of this year's Intergalactic Space Race is . . .

the rocket racing car!"

"Well done, Riley," said Jack,
"I think you found our super booster button!"
The Martian handed a trophy to Jack. "Congratulations! And
thank you for helping us all! Three cheers for Miraculous Mechanic Jack!"
All the aliens were clapping and chanting Jack's name.

Soon it was time for Jack and Riley to go home.
They said goodbye to their new friends, jumped into the car,
and streaked through space back to Rally Road workshop.

"Phew! What an adventure, Riley.
This car really is the ultimate racing machine!

And look what I've found – SUPERSONIC Space Chews
for a SUPERSONIC dog!"

For Lucy

– AR

For My Wifey

– MB

SIMON AND SCHUSTER

First published in Great Britain in 2012 by Simon and Schuster UK Ltd

1st Floor, 222 Gray's Inn Road, London WC1X 8HB

A CBS Company

Text copyright © 2012 Alison Ritchie

Illustrations copyright © 2012 Mike Byrne

Concept © 2012 Simon and Schuster UK

The right of Alison Ritchie and Mike Byrne to be identified

as the author and illustrator of this work has been asserted by them

in accordance with the Copyright, Designs and Patents Act, 1988

A CIP catalogue record for this book is available from the British Library upon request

ISBN: 978 0 85707 567 3

Printed in China

1 3 5 7 9 10 8 6 4 2

**Look out for more of
Jack's amazing adventures,
coming soon to a bookshop near you!**

**Jack's Mega Machines:
Dinosaur Digger**

**Jack's Mega Machines:
Supersonic Submarine**

**Jack's Mega Machines:
Mighty Monster Truck**